KNOCK KNOCK KNOCK KNOCK KNOCK
KNOCK KNOCK KNOCK KNOCK KNOCK
KNOCK KNOCK KNOCK KNOCK KNOCK
KNOCK KNOCK KNOCK KNOCK KNOCK
KNOCK KNOCK KNOCK KNOCK
KNOCK KNOCK KNOCK KNOCK
KNOCK KNOCK KNOCK KNOCK
KNOCK KNOCK KNOCK KNOCK
KNOCK KNOCK KNOCK KNOCK
KNOCK KNOCK KNOCK KNOCK
KNOCK KNOCK KNOCK KNOCK KNOCK
KNOCK KNOCK KNOCK KNOCK KNOCK
KNOCK KNOCK KNOCK KNOCK KNOCK
KNOCK KNOCK KNOCK KNOCK KNOCK
KNOCK KNOCK KNOCK KNOCK KNOCK
KNOCK KNOCK KNOCK KNOCK KNOCK
KNOCK KNOCK KNOCK KNOCK

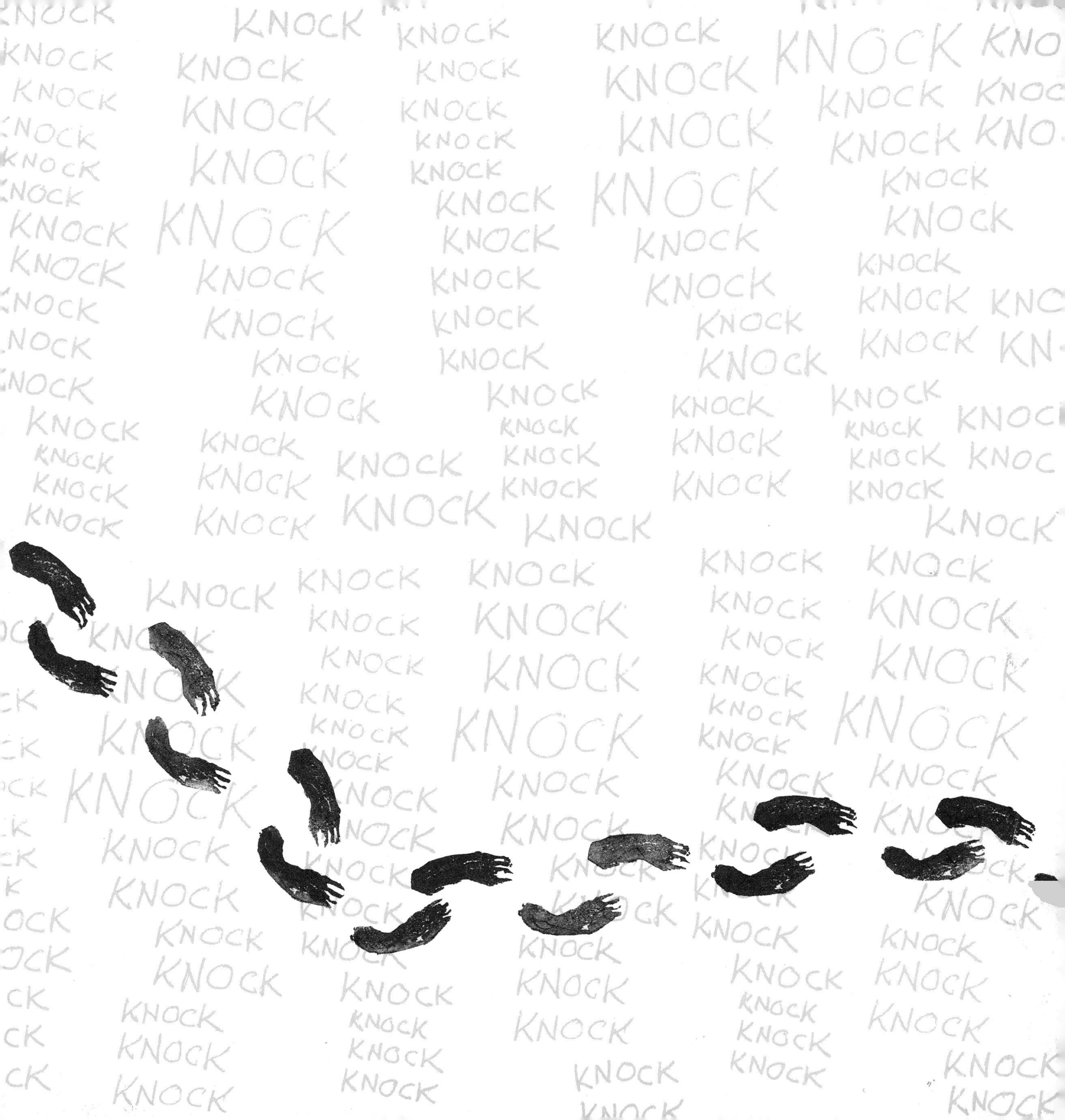

Possum Come a-Knockin'

by NANCY VAN LAAN

Illustrated by GEORGE BOOTH

Alfred A. Knopf, New York

For John, Celia, Rachel, Jessica, and
all my kinfolk way down South   —N.V.L.

To Grover Babcock, my brother-in-law,
who loves critters   —G.B.

THIS IS A BORZOI BOOK PUBLISHED BY ALFRED A. KNOPF, INC.

Copyright © 1990 by Nancy Van Laan
Illustrations copyright © 1990 by George Booth
All rights reserved under International and Pan-American Copyright
Conventions. Published in the United States by Alfred A. Knopf, Inc., New
York, and simultaneously in Canada by Random House of Canada Limited,
Toronto. Distributed by Random House, Inc., New York.
Book design by Mina Greenstein
Manufactured in Singapore
10 9 8 7 6 5 4 3 2 1

19 0856

Library of Congress Cataloging-in-Publication Data
Van Laan, Nancy. Possum come a-knockin'. Summary: A cumulative tale
in verse about a mysterious stranger that interrupts a family's daily
routine. [1. Family Life—Fiction. 2. Opossums—Fiction. 3. Stories in
rhyme] I. Booth, George, 1926– ill. II. Title. PZ8.3.V34Po 1990 [E]
88-12751 ISBN 0-394-82206-4 ISBN 0-394-92206-9 (lib. bdg.)

Possum come a-knockin'
at the door, at the door.
Possum come a-knockin'
at the door.

Granny was a-sittin'
and a-rockin' and a-knittin'
when a possum come a-knockin'
at the door.

Ma was busy cookin'
in the kitchen makin' taters
when a possum come a-knockin'
at the door.

Pa was busy fixin'
and a-bangin' and a-poundin'
when a possum come a-knockin'
at the door.

Pappy was a-whittlin',
makin' play toys for the baby,
when a possum come a-knockin'
at the door.

Sis was tossin' Baby
while Pappy was a-whittlin'
when a possum come a-knockin'
at the door.

Brother was untanglin'
all the twiny line for fishin'
while Sis was tossin' Baby
and Pappy was a-whittlin'

and Pa was busy fixin'
and Ma was busy cookin'
and Granny was a-knittin'
when a possum come a-knockin'
at the door.

Coon-dawg was a-twitchin'
and a-scratchin' in the corner
when a possum come a-knockin'
at the door.

Tom-cat started sniffin'
and a-spittin' and a-hissin'
when a possum come a-knockin'
at the door.

"What's that?" Sis said.
"Don't know," Brother said.
"What's that?" Pa said.
"Don't know," Granny said.
"But that cat!" she said.
"That cat oughter go!"

Then dawg started sniffin'
and a-pawin' and a-growlin'
while the cat, tail a-twitchin',
was a-hissin' and a-howlin',

makin' Granny stop a-knittin'
and Pappy stop a-whittlin'
and Baby start a-fussin',
Sis and Brother start a-cussin',
'cause a li'l ol' possum
was a-knockin'
at the door.

"What's that?" Granny said.
"Don't know," Pappy said.
"What's that?" Ma said.
"Don't know," Pa said.
Then I creepy-crossed the floor
and peeked under the door.

"It's a possum come a-knockin'
on the door!" I said.
"It's a possum come a-knockin'
on the door!"

Then Brother came a-leapin'
and Sis came a-runnin'
and Baby came a-crawlin'
and dawg started howlin'
and Pappy was a-chucklin'
and Granny's eyes was twinklin'
as Ma followed Pa to the door.

"Now, hush!" Pa said.
"Now, hush!" Ma said.
And slowly Pa opened
up the door.
"Now, y'all stop your hollerin',
your fussin', and your cussin',
'cause there's nothin'
that's a-knockin' at the door."

"No possum?" Pappy said.
"No possum," Pa said.
"No possum?" Granny said.
"No possum," Ma said.
  Then we all started doin'
  like before.

Granny was a-sittin'
while Pappy was a-whittlin'.
Ma was a-cookin'
while Pa was a-fixin'.

Brother was untanglin'
while Sis was tossin' Baby.
Coon-dawg was a-scratchin'
while Tom-cat was a-lickin'.

And I was just a-sittin'
and a-lookin' out the winder
when I saw what I saw
scoot up the old oak tree.

A possum was a-scootin'
and a-scramblin' and a-danglin'.
That possum that was knockin'
made a fool out of me!

KNOCK KNOCK KNOCK KNOCK KNOCK KNOCK
KNOCK KNOCK KNOCK KNOCK KNOCK KNOCK
KNOCK KNOCK KNOCK KNOCK KNOCK KNOCK
KNOCK KNOCK KNOCK KNOCK KNOCK KNOCK
KNOCK KNOCK KNOCK KNOCK KNOCK KNOCK
KNOCK KNOCK KNOCK KNOCK KNOCK KNOCK
KNOCK KNOCK KNOCK KNOCK KNOCK KNOCK
KNOCK KNOCK KNOCK KNOCK KNOCK KNOCK
KNOCK KNOCK KNOCK KNOCK KNOCK KNOCK
KNOCK KNOCK KNOCK KNOCK KNOCK KNOCK
KNOCK KNOCK KNOCK KNOCK KNOCK KNOCK
KNOCK KNOCK KNOCK KNOCK KNOCK KNOCK
KNOCK KNOCK KNOCK KNOCK KNOCK KNOCK
KNOCK KNOCK KNOCK KNOCK KNOCK KNOCK
KNOCK KNOCK KNOCK KNOCK KNOCK KNOCK
KNOCK KNOCK KNOCK KNOCK KNOCK KNOCK

KNOCK KNOCK